Aki's Special Gift

by Winston White

illustrated by Yu Cha Pak

 HOUGHTON MIFFLIN   BOSTON

crib

Aki had a new baby brother, Yoshi.
She wanted to give him a special gift.

She wanted to give Yoshi a rattle.
But Aunt Suzu gave Yoshi a rattle.

She wanted to give Yoshi a teddy bear.
But Uncle Kento gave Yoshi a teddy bear.

She wanted to give Yoshi a blanket.
But Cousin Misako gave Yoshi a blanket.

Aki asked her grandfather, "What gift can I give Yoshi?"

"You don't have to buy a gift, Aki," Grandfather said. "You can make one. I'll show you how."

paper

Grandfather told Aki about origami. "Origami is part of our Japanese culture," he said. "It's a way of making things by folding paper. You can make a flower, a butterfly, or a bird with paper."

Grandfather showed Aki how to make a bird.
Then he showed her how to fold the paper to
make a flower.

They made many things together. They
made a butterfly, a frog, and even a strawberry.

"Now you have many gifts for Yoshi,"
Grandfather said.

wood

string

Aki had an idea. She got two strips of wood
and some string.

Aki tied the strips of wood together. Then
she tied each of the paper shapes with string.

"See what I made for Yoshi, Grandfather! I'll hang it over his bed," said Aki.

"Oh, Aki," said Grandfather. "It's a very special gift!"

Aki was very happy. She couldn't wait for
Yoshi to get bigger. She would teach him all
about origami!